GHOST STORIES OF OLD TEXAS, III

By
Zinita Fowler

Illustrated by
J. Kay Wilson

EAKIN PRESS ⟁ Fort Worth, Texas
www.EakinPress.com

Copyright © 1995
By Zinita Fowler
Published By Eakin Press
An Imprint of Wild Horse Media Group
P.O. Box 331779
Fort Worth, Texas 76163
1-817-344-7036
www.EakinPress.com
ALL RIGHTS RESERVED
1 2 3 4 5 6 7 8 9
Paperback ISBN 978-1-68179-248-4
eBook ISBN 978-1-68179-324-5

Library of Congress Cataloging-in-Publication Data

Fowler, Zinita.
    Ghost stories of old Texas, III / by Zinita Fowler. — 1st ed.
        p.   cm.
    Summary: A collection of eighteen ghostly tales illustrating the cultural heritage of Texas.
    ISBN 978-1-68179-248-4
    1. Ghosts — Texas. 2. Tales — Texas. [1. Ghosts — Folklore.
    2. Folklore — Texas.] I. Title.
    PZ8.1.F818GK   1995
    398.2--dc20
                                                    95-37431
                                                        CIP
                                                        AC

Contents

Contents

iii

Preface

Since 1983 when *Ghost Stories of Old Texas* came out, I have crisscrossed the state of Texas, telling my stories to hundreds of schoolchildren. They have been a most appreciative audience. I can truthfully say that I have never encountered a lack of interest or anything but enthusiasm and participation.

I credit this response to the stories in my books. First off, they are ghost stories — an instant favorite with children. But more in their favor is that they are *Texas* ghost stories, garnered from the vast storehouse of Texas folklore. This gives them a certain authenticity, a realness, if you will.

At nearly every session, in the quietness which follows the telling of an eerie or poignant tale, a wide-eyed child will whisper, "Did that *really* happen?"

My answer: "Maybe so, maybe not. It's for you to decide."

*To all these good folks who aided and abetted me
while I was chasing ghosts all over Texas, I'd like
to say, "I thank you most kindly."*

> *Dr. Jim Conrad*
> *Melissa and Tom Baker*
> *Nancy Schmidt*
> *Finley Stewart*

> *Teachers and students of:*
> *Celina ISD*
> *Geronimo ISD*
> *Gregory-Portland ISD*

The Haunted Restaurant

There are three of them. Elizabeth, the youngest, is gentle and kind and sometimes very sad. Caroline is the feisty senior, who sometimes has temper fits and throws things. And Will is an overall-clad farmer, who doesn't have much of a personality and just seems to be there.

These spirits reside at the Catfish Plantation cafe in Waxahachie. This converted Victorian-style house that sits in a grove of trees on Water Street was built as a private home in 1895.

Melissa and Tom Baker bought the house in 1984, with plans to open a cafe and serve Cajun-style food. It was not long before strange things began happening.

Melissa went into the house one morning to find a fresh pot of coffee steaming in the kitchen. She had the only key to the restaurant, but thought perhaps someone had managed to get in to pull an early-morning trick. As it turned out, this was only the beginning of the tricks.

1

A week or two later, Melissa found a large tea urn in the middle of the kitchen floor with all the teacups stacked inside. Sometimes things would fall off shelves without reason and the radio would change stations all by itself.

Employees began to tell about strange things that happened when they were on the job — coffee cups flying across the room, doors opening and closing unexpectedly, and lights flickering on and off. They also noticed sudden cold spots in just one part of the room.

At first, the Bakers said little about these mysterious things, fearing it might hurt their business. Finally, they allowed a parapsychologist from Dallas to do research on their uninvited guests. Her findings made it all quite clear.

Elizabeth Anderson lived in the house when it was built in 1895. As a young girl, she was engaged to be married. There is some confusion about her story. Some say that in an arranged marriage she was to marry an older man, although she loved another. On her wedding night, she either took her own life or was murdered by her jilted sweetheart. Either way, the fact is that she died violently of strangulation.

Elizabeth's presence is felt most often in the main dining room. She likes to stand near the diners and touch them on the arm or shoulder — a sort of cool, tingling sensation like a mild electric shock. Guests have actually seen her standing in a front bay window, wearing her wedding finery.

Caroline Mooney, another resident of the house,

2

died of a stroke in 1970 at the age of eighty-two. Today, guests claim to see her wearing old-fashioned black clothing.

She has a hot temper and gets blamed for the flying china and slamming doors. She was a teetotaler and has no patience with the consumption of alcohol in any form. Although the Plantation does not serve liquor, guests are allowed to bring their own. Caroline sometimes expresses her disapproval of this practice by sending wine glasses crashing to the floor. The cooks also blame her when guests complain of too much salt in the bread pudding.

One day a car load of visitors pulled up in the rear parking lot. They saw an elderly woman in a long black dress standing at the open back door. She was making sweeping gestures with her arm, inviting them to come inside. They waved at her but went on to the front entrance. When they asked their waitress who the old woman at the back door was, they were told that no one like that worked at the Catfish Plantation.

Will, the third ghost, occupied the house during the Depression in the 1930s. He doesn't do much of anything and is most often sighted standing on the porch in his work clothes. Occasionally, he expresses his appreciation for a pretty girl by giving her a little pat on the behind. He also contributes to the cold spots.

These are friendly spirits. When Caroline goes on a tear, she does a few dollars worth of damage, but patrons are never harmed. Melissa Baker admits that when she is alone in the building and realizes she has ghostly company, it does make her a bit uncomfortable. Sometimes, she leaves the cafe and goes on home.

As for the fear that the presence of ghosts would hurt business, quite the opposite has happened. Since the Bakers made public their extended family, business has picked up considerably. In fact, most diners at the restaurant seem to enjoy the knowledge that something unusual might happen while they are there.

The Bakers have collected a notebook full of ghostly things their patrons have experienced at the Plantation. Rather than being put off by eating in a haunted place, it could be said that these folks really got into the "spirit" of the thing.

4

Tiny Ghostly Fingers

The railroad crossing at Villa Main Street just outside San Antonio used to be extremely dangerous. The tracks were at the top of a steep grade, and the Model T and Model A cars of the period often stalled in the worst possible place, right on the tracks.

One night, the engine of an old pickup truck died at the top of the grade. There was no time for the five small children riding in the bed of the truck to escape from an oncoming train, and they were killed.

From that time on, a strange thing began to occur at the crossing. Drivers of cars that stalled on the tracks felt themselves being pushed slowly forward, out of danger. Once safe, when they got out to thank the Good Samaritan who had possibly saved their lives, no one was there.

Word spread throughout the city, and a group of teens decided to find out for themselves just what was going on. They drove their old jalopy onto the

5

tracks and deliberately stalled the motor. Nothing happened until they heard the whistle of an approaching train.

Before the driver could get the engine going, the young people felt their car slowly moving forward, out of harm's way. As the train roared past, they leaped out to find whoever or whatever had pushed the car. Like others before them, they found nothing.

Now their curiosity was really aroused. They were determined to find out what caused the cars to move off the tracks, even if their own car got demolished in the effort. Again, they drove out to the crossing, and again, they stalled their car on the tracks. This time, however, they heavily dusted the rear bumper of the car with white powder. Then, they hid in bushes alongside the tracks to see for themselves what was happening.

Far down the track, they saw the headlight of the approaching train, and they heard the whistle sounding nearer and nearer. They found it hard to believe when the car began to move slowly forward and then coasted down the grade as the train hurtled by.

The young people fell over one another in their eagerness to get to the car, and what they found there caused them to gasp in shock. In the powder on the rear bumper were five different sets of small hand- and fingerprints.

The crossing is still there, but it is not as dangerous. The grade is not so steep, and the powerful engines of today's cars have no problem getting safely across the tracks.

But many people in San Antonio will tell you they have witnessed the strange occurrence at the Villa Main Street crossing, and many school children are able to finish the story once it is started. As with all ghost legends, there are several versions, but what is most appealing in all the stories is that the spirits of the little slain children are trying to keep others from meeting the same fate.

Pretty Peggy

The boys crouched in the tall grass at the edge of Graham Park. They strained their eyes to see the house sitting by itself in the still darkness. It was an attractive old place with six tall columns and a wide porch stretching across the entire front of the house. No one else was around. Only the chirping sound of night insects broke the silence. The boys were up to no good.

"Ya'll stay here," whispered the leader. "I'll go look in the window and see what's up."

He slipped away and moved toward the house, staying in the shadows of the trees. For a time, a long time to those who were waiting in the grass, there was absolute quiet.

Suddenly, the silence was split by a terrified scream, followed by the pounding of running feet. The boys stood up as their leader dashed by, yelling, "C'mon! Let's get out of here!"

A short while later in a deserted garage where the boys had made their headquarters, the leader was finally able to get himself together enough to tell the others what happened.

"It was awful!" he declared. "When I got close to the house, I could hear this whiny little voice, like a little kid and it was sort of singin', 'Pretty Peggy, Pretty Peggy'—over and over."

He stopped for a moment, breathing hard. "Well, I slipped over to the window and looked in and—I ain't lyin'—there was this little old wooden doll sittin' in a rockin' chair by the fireplace and it was rockin' back and forth and sort of singin' to itself."

"Aw," broke in one of the others, "that could've been one of them mechanical—"

"You hush up!" the first boy said fiercely. "There's more. It was like that little old doll knew I was at the window, 'cause all of a sudden, it stopped rockin' and singin' and *it looked right at me.* Its eyes was sort of glittery and *mean.* And then, that doll got up and started walkin'—comin' toward me—and I seen that it didn't hardly have no face at all. I yelled at it to make it stay away and then I got out of there. I ain't *never* goin' back to that park again. Nothin' could make me!"

This is a story that has been passed down from one generation of children to another in the Hunt County seat of Greenville in northeast Texas. It is based on facts. The house in Graham Park is the old Ende homeplace, built by an early Greenville settler, Fred Ende, in 1859.

Ende was quite a businessman. In addition to his home, he built a general store on the courthouse square and later a three-story brick hotel.

9

Although he spent a lot of time on his business affairs, Fred Ende was a good family man. During the Civil War, things got very tight in the South and it was hard for Ende to get stock for his store. In 1863, when his three-year-old daughter, Louise, asked for a doll for Christmas, there were none to be found from any of the merchants for miles around.

Determined not to disappoint the little girl, Ende found a piece of heart pine and whittled out the head of a doll. He painted the face and hair, and his wife made the body and clothing from scraps of cotton and lace she had saved through the years.

It turned out to be a beautiful doll. Louise named it "Peggy" and carried it with her everywhere she went. She bestowed so many affectionate hugs and kisses on the little wooden doll that after a few years, the face was almost worn away. Only the bright blue eyes continued to stare unblinking at the world.

After Louise grew up, married and had children of her own, the Ende home was given to the Hunt County Historical Society. It was moved to Graham Park and made into a small museum. Peggy, seated in a rocking chair, had a place of honor by the fireplace.

After an incident of vandalism which caused some minor damage to the home, the story of "Pretty Peggy" surfaced. Whether there is any truth to the legend of a walking, talking doll who is fiercely protective of its home, or whether it is simply a ghostly yarn invented to keep any mischief makers away from the old Ende house, it seems to have done its job well.

The Waiting Maiden

Near the little town of San Gabriel, not far from the San Gabriel River, are the ruins of a once beautiful old ranch house. It was the home of a lovely girl, the only child of a prominent ranching family and the apple of her father's eye.

During the roundup one year, she was riding her pony out near the river and stopped to watch a cowboy chasing a stray calf back to the herd. She noticed the skillful way he handled his horse and the careful way he guided the little lost animal back to its mother.

She boldly rode over to him. "You are a very fine rider," she called out.

The cowboy wheeled around to face her, and when he saw that it was the ranch owner's daughter, he swept off his hat and stammered, *"Gracias, señorita."*

The girl fell speechless as she looked at the handsome young man. His eyes were dark and thickly-lashed, and his hair was black and curly. She knew she wanted to know him better, but there was a problem. He was a Mexican, and her father would never grant permission for him to call on her. In those days girls of her status in society did not mingle socially with persons of other races.

This, however, was a young woman who was accustomed to having what she wanted. She told the cowboy that she walked by the river every evening at sunset. Then, she turned her pony and galloped away.

Dressed in her most attractive clothes, the girl strolled down to the river in the late afternoon. Soon, she saw the cowboy on the other side of the river. He walked on a tree trunk that stretched across the river like a footbridge, and in a moment, he was by her side. Something electric seemed to flash between the young couple, and it was true love at first sight.

They walked together under the trees, learning as much as they could about each other. Thereafter, they met at the river every chance they had. The cowboy always approached from the opposite bank and ran nimbly across the trunk. He came by this route in hopes that no one would become suspicious.

As the days grew shorter and the air cooler, the sweethearts knew they would have to make other plans. Soon, it would be too cold to meet by the river. The girl knew that if her father discovered her secret, he would forbid her to ever see her lover again. The couple decided to run away together.

On the day they planned to leave it began to rain. For a solid week, heavy downpours beat upon the roof of the ranch house. The girl stared out the window toward the river, her heart aching for the sight of her sweetheart.

Finally, when the rain stopped, the girl slipped away from the house and hurried on eager feet to the riverbank. She was dismayed to see the usually placid San Gabriel turned into a rushing torrent of ugly brown water, only inches below the footbridge.

The cowboy appeared on the other side. Calling, "Ah, *mia Cara!*" he stepped out onto the fallen tree and began to hurry across. In his haste, he failed to realize that the rain had made the footbridge slippery. Before the girl's horrified eyes, the cowboy lost his footing and fell into the raging water. He was swept downstream.

When the girl did not return to the ranch house by nightfall, her father went out to look for her. When he found her, she was wandering up and down the riverbank, crying and calling out the name of her lover. Her father spoke to her, and she looked at him with empty eyes, not recognizing him.

Even though the rancher called in doctors from all over the world, the lovely girl was diagnosed incurably insane. Every evening at sunset, she would wander down to the riverbank to meet her sweetheart. She would hold out her arms to him and then scream in horror as she relived the terrible tragedy.

Her father was heartbroken. He knew that his beloved daughter had been afraid to confess her love for a Mexican cowboy, and he was ashamed and sorrowful.

She died a few short months after the cowboy drowned, some say of a broken heart. Her father buried her beside the riverbank by the fallen tree where she had been so happy. Now, many old-timers say that if you go down by the river at sunset, you can hear the whispering of the two lovers. Sometimes, you can see the drooping figure of a young girl, waiting in vain for her sweetheart to return.

A Message From Mack

No one knew who she was or where she came from. She simply showed up one day in 1885 in the little Panhandle town of Tascosa on the arm of Mickey McCormick.

Mickey was the popular owner of a livery stable in the small town. Although his business was booming and he knew everyone in town, not much was known about Mickey. He was Irish, handsome, friendly and a bachelor, he never talked about his past.

Mickey liked to gamble. Every week or so, he drove his four-wheeled buggy over to the gaming tables of the dance halls in the nearby army town of Mobeetie. He returned from one of these trips with a girl. He introduced this beautiful, dark-haired girl as Elizabeth.

The townspeople were curious about Elizabeth. She spoke as though she had a good education, carried herself straight and proud like a woman of high birth, and wore expensive-looking dresses made of

15

fine materials. Her curly hair was dark, but her eyes were a bright blue, and she spoke with an accent.

Bits of information came to the Tascosa residents from cowboys who drifted through the town on cattle drives. Elizabeth was better known to them as "Frenchy," a dance hall girl. They said she was a runaway from a wealthy family in New Orleans and had been on the vaudeville stage for awhile before coming to Mobeetie. She wouldn't tell anyone her name, so they nicknamed her Frenchy because of her accent.

When asked about her past Elizabeth's answer was always, "No one will ever find out who I am." No one did, except perhaps Mickey, and he was as close-mouthed as Frenchy.

Mickey built a little two-room adobe house near the livery stable, and the couple began their life together. When Mickey drove his four-wheeled buggy to Mobeetie to gamble, Frenchy went with him. She was skillful at the card games, and often came away with more money than he did.

They were always together, except when Mickey had to drive a customer on a long trip. Even then, he sent a letter to his love every chance he had. When she received his letters, Frenchy would stand beneath a twisted old cottonwood tree that grew in front of the little adobe house, waving it at passersby.

"I heard from Mack today," she would call, a bright smile on her face. Mack was her pet name for Mickey, but he always called her Elizabeth.

With the passing years, the little town of Tascosa fell on hard times. The railroad passed it by and so the herds of cattle with their cowboys no longer came through. People began to move away.

But Mickey and Frenchy stayed. They loved their little house with its cottonwood tree, their hunting dogs, and their life together. The livery stable closed for lack of trade, but Mickey kept the four-wheeled buggy and every so often had a hauling job. The sound of the wheels on the road could be heard, sometimes late at night, coming home.

Mickey was considerably older than Frenchy, and eventually his health began to fail. He died in 1921, and Frenchy buried him near a little house on a hill so she could see the marker on his grave from her window. No family or relatives came to the funeral; only Frenchy and Mickey's friends were there.

As Tascosa grew smaller and the little house more isolated and worn down, friends begged Frenchy to move to Channing, a larger town twenty miles away. "I need to be with my Mack," she would say with a bright smile.

So she lived on alone in the little house. But was she really alone? The few people who still lived in Tascosa often got up in the morning, realizing they had heard the sound of Mickey's buggy wheels on the road late at night. And if they went to check on Frenchy, as they often did, they would find her out beneath the old cottonwood tree, a happy smile on her face.

"I heard from Mack," she would say.

17

The Headless
Boy of Geronimo

When the Neuman family moved into a big two-story house on the main street of the little town of Geronimo in 1905, they were told that "someone" or "something" already lived there.

"The house is haunted," the person who was moving out said. "I'm afraid to stay here any longer."

The Neumans laughed at him. They had strong Christian beliefs and didn't think such things as ghosts or spirits existed. They moved into the house and settled down.

There were two strange things about the house. One of a pair of double doors leading from the front porch into the hall could not be opened. It was not locked, but even Mr. Neuman, who was a strong man, could not force it open. There were also cold spots in the house that could not be explained. Most of these were in the master bedroom.

The Neuman family refused to read anything supernatural into these things. They just assumed that the foundation had shifted through the years, causing the door to wedge tighter into the frame and cracks to occur, allowing cold drafts to seep in.

One night, two of the daughters went outside to bring the washing in off the line. Suddenly, they heard a loud noise like the barking of a dog that drew their attention to a brush pile by the windmill. They were startled to see a small white form emerge from the brush and head in their direction. They dropped the clothes and ran into the house.

When they told their mother what they had seen, she told them it was probably just a shaft of moonlight reflected off the blades of the windmill, and scolded them for dropping the clothes on the ground.

A few nights later, an older sister who was visiting went out on the porch to soak her feet in a pan of water. She, too, heard the noise from the brush pile and saw the small white form. Her sisters had told her about their sighting, so she sat very still and continued to watch.

The white shape formed itself into the figure of a little boy who climbed up on the brush pile and began to jump up and down and dance in the moonlight. He was wearing shoes that were too big for his feet, and he made strange barking noises as he played his little games.

Suddenly, the little boy stopped moving and stood very still as though he realized he was being watched. Then, he leaped off the brush pile and began to move swiftly toward the house. The sister screamed and ran when she saw that the ghostly child had no head!

The parents still maintained their attitude that no such thing existed. But if it did, they didn't need to fear it. If the girls believed there was a ghostly little boy, then they should pray for his soul.

One night, a large group of church members were at the Neuman house for choir practice. The one double door was open to cool the house. Suddenly, the other door crashed open, and there, in the hallway, stood the little boy.

There was an instant of shocked silence as everyone stared at the small figure, which was beyond a doubt the one the Neuman sisters had seen. He was even wearing the oversized shoes.

Only one thing was different. This child had a head, covered with thick, curly blond hair. And he carried a pillow case under his arms.

Before anyone could respond the little boy ran down the hall and up the stairs. They followed him, but he was nowhere to be found. They searched the house and yard, and the nearby fields and woods, but the vision was never seen again.

The Neuman family continued to live in the house for thirteen more years. No one could ever explain who the little boy was, where he came from, and why he might have been residing in the old house. He has become a local legend that sends chills up the spines of school children on moonlit nights.

The Woman
Who Refuses to Die

In the little town of Honey Island, north of Beaumont, there once lived a rich woman by the name of Hannah Brown. Her husband had died, leaving her a life insurance policy worth ten thousand dollars. With shrewd investments and some pure luck, Hannah parlayed her small nest egg into a fortune.

She built a three-story mansion with a many-columned porch and large, airy rooms furnished in velvet brocade, and fine wood. She rode around in a fancy carriage drawn by high-stepping white horses with plumes on their heads.

Hannah also bought precious jewels of all kinds — diamonds, rubies, emeralds, sapphires — and had them fashioned into necklaces, bracelets, and rings. She loved her jewelry better than anything else in the world. Rumor was that she slept in it, never taking it off.

As she grew older, Hannah got very selfish. She didn't want to share what she had with anyone else.

A will was drawn up in which she stated that she was to be buried wearing her favorite pieces of jewelry and all the rest would be put in her jewelry box and placed between her hands.

She died at the age of eighty and was buried with much mourning — more, perhaps, for the treasure being interred with her than for Hannah. In truth, she had been a most unpleasant woman and her own family cared very little for her.

Hannah had been in the ground only a few days when her grave was invaded by a group of young ruffians, intent on getting the precious jewels in her coffin. Imagine their surprise when, after throwing open the lid of the box, they saw Hannah staring at them with a wide grin on her face. When she sat up, pointed at them, and demanded what they were doing there, the grave robbers ran away as fast as they could. It was said that the hair of one of the youths turned snow white in a few hours. Not one of them was ever the same after that.

Hannah's sister and niece moved into her mansion on the day of the funeral, and they had been having a high old time entertaining their friends and throwing wild parties.

On the night she spooked the grave robbers, Hannah also appeared at the head of the great staircase in the grand hall of her house. She pointed down at her sister and niece, who were cowering on the floor below. In a low, menacing voice, she said one word, "Out!"

The two terrified women backed away from the

22

fiery, accusing eyes, and once they reached the double French doors, they turned and bolted away into the woods. They never returned even to pick up their own belongings.

The big house is still there in Honey Island. No one lives there, unless you count the widow Brown, who seems to enjoy walking around the house with diamonds and rubies sparkling on her neck, arms, and fingers. You might even catch a glimpse of her through one of the big picture windows. That's if you believe in such things.

The Phantom Light of Old Fort Stockton

Indians were seldom seen inside the walls of old Fort Stockton. Occasionally, one young brave accompanied a Kiowa chief on missions of peace to the fort. The boy proudly walked the streets of the fort, looking neither to the right nor left, with eyes as cold and dark as agate. That is, until they fell on the slender form of the lovely Francesca, daughter of one of the captains at the fort.

Fort Stockton was one of many outposts built by the government in the mid-1800s in an effort to control the roving bands of Comanches and Kiowas. These tribes were hunters and never stayed in one spot very long. They played a game of cat-and-mouse with both the federal and state governments, talking peace but stealing horses and killing settlers when the occasion arose.

West Texas was dangerous country in those days, but it was safe enough inside the fort. Many of the officers brought their families with them when the fort was completed and moved them into living quarters inside the walls.

Life could be exciting for a beautiful young girl like Francesca who had most of the single men stationed at the fort wanting to marry her. She was also very aware that the eyes of the tall Indian brave who appeared now and then fell on her with favor, even showing signs of warmth and tenderness.

Francesca had already decided who she wanted. Unfortunately, he could not return her affections, for he was Ferenor, nephew of the priest of the garrison church and planning to enter the priesthood himself.

In such a small, enclosed community as a military outpost, it was inevitable that the two young people would meet often. As he went about his duties during the church services, Ferenor was aware of the girl's yearning glances, making his heart beat faster. She was so lovely, so fragile and sweet, and so irresistible. Ferenor fell in love, and he fell hard. He would abandon his plan to become a priest and marry Francesca instead.

However, it was not that simple. When the young couple informed the priest of his nephew's change in plans, he flew into a rage. He called their love for each other evil and pagan and ordered them out of the church, not caring that a terrible storm was howling with fury, whipping the countryside with wind and rain. The door slammed behind the unhappy sweethearts, leaving them in the dark and cold.

They started for Francesca's quarters, but the storm beat about them so fiercely that they lost their way. Fighting the wind and soaked to the skin, they took a wrong turn and found themselves in the woods, outside the fort. Francesca sank to the ground, exhausted and frightened.

"I can go no further," she sobbed.

Ferenor knelt beside the girl and put his arms about her, doing his best to shelter her from the storm. The rain slackened a bit and when Ferenor looked up, he saw a light, flickering in the distance.

"Francesca, we're saved!" he cried. "That must be a settler's cabin."

He scooped the girl up in his arms and started toward the light. But it was gone. There was no cabin. Ferenor strained his eyes to see through the rain, and once again, he spotted a light as though from a flickering lamp in a cabin window.

He realized that his fragile beloved could go no farther, so he found a large rock which afforded her some shelter and knelt for a moment beside her.

"Stay here, darling," he whispered to her. "I'll get some help and be back very soon."

Again, he started toward the light, and again, it was gone. Then, it appeared in another spot, and Ferenor headed for it again. The light moved here and there, seeming to taunt him, and Ferenor chased it desperately, going deeper and deeper into the forest.

The ground underfoot was slippery and treacherous, and several times, the boy slipped to his knees, but each time he got up, sobbing in frustration. Then, he fell, and rolled down a sharp incline, hitting his head against a rock and slipping into unconsciousness.

For a long time, he lay there and when consciousness finally returned, the rain had stopped. Frantically, he got to his feet and looked about him. He didn't know where he was nor where he had left his sweetheart.

"Francesca!" he called, again and again, running through the woods. "Francesca! Where are you?"

Neither of the young lovers was ever seen again. The soldiers from the fort searched for days, but the rain had washed away any traces of where they might be. It was assumed, sadly, that they had been captured or killed by the Indians.

All that is left of the old fort today are some old abandoned buildings of adobe and limestone and a few crumbling walls. On stormy nights, there are those who say that through the howling wind and pouring rain, they can hear the mournful cry of the lost Ferenor calling to his beloved, "Francesca! Francesca!" And sometimes the voice seems to come and go, following a light that flickers here and there through the old ruins like a will-o'-the-wisp, beckoning the poor lost lover to his doom.

Some storytellers say that it was the lovesick Indian brave who lured Ferenor into the forest to kill him. Then he carried Francesca back to his camp. Since he knew the land around the fort very well, it would have been easy for him to show a light, perhaps a piece of burning wood, here and there to confuse the lost young man. This would explain the disappearance of the lovers, but not the pitiful calls and the flickering light people of today declare they have heard and seen.

The Ghost Horses
of Palo Duro Canyon

Out near Amarillo there is a deep, rugged gorge in the earth that some folks call the Texas Grand Canyon. Its proper name is the Palo Duro Canyon, and it played a big part in the history of West Texas.

Today, Palo Duro Canyon is a tourist attraction for its scenic beauty and a staging area for the outdoor musical production of "Texas" each summer. According to old-timers in the area, it is also the scene of another type awe-inspiring sight. This one happens only on bright moonlit nights and only true believers in the spirit of the past have ever claimed a sighting.

It begins with a noise like distant thunder that comes closer and closer until it can be identified as the sound of hundreds of hooves pounding against the rock-hard soil around the canyon. And then in the moonlight, it comes into view — a herd of beautiful horses racing at breakneck speed along the canyon's rim. They have almost transparent, silky

manes with tails flung backward and eyes flashing like jewels as they race by.

And then suddenly they are gone as though whisked away by the warm West Texas wind. The silence is intense and much more eerie than the sight of the ghostly stallions.

It is a matter of history that in September of 1874, Palo Duro Canyon was the site of a battle between Col. Ranald S. MacKenzie's 4th Cavalry and a gathering of Kiowa, Comanche, and Cheyenne Indians. The chiefs, Maman-ti, Lone Wolf, and Quannah Parker had camped their people on the floor of the canyon. They were weary from being pursued for months by the soldiers and felt they would be safe there with the steep canyon walls protecting them. Also, there was water and pasture land for their hundreds of horses. It proved to be more a trap than a refuge.

Colonel MacKenzie's men descended single-file into the canyon under cover of night and caught the Indians by surprise. Most of them were able to escape, but the soldiers rounded up all the horses and burned the camp and all supplies.

There were more than a thousand horses and mules, some of them in poor condition. MacKenzie and his scouts and guides picked out the animals considered fit enough to be worth saving. The rest were shot to make certain the Indians would never get them back. They knew without horses, the Plains Indians were helpless.

The dead horses were piled into several stacks

and allowed to rot in the hot Texas sun until only the bones were left. In time, they turned white and seemed to serve as a sort of gravestone for Indian power in the West. Finally, the bones were carted away, and only the sad West Texas wind was left to mourn the fate of Kiowa, Comanche, and Cheyenne.

And then, the sightings of the ghost herd began. Very few have claimed to see the magnificent animals, but the legend persists. Perhaps we are not meant to forget what happened to the Indians camped in Palo Duro Canyon and to the horses that were their life.

The Crazy Courthouse Clock

The picturesque little town of Gonzales in South Texas was the scene of a stirring incident in Texas history. The Mexican army approached the townspeople and demanded that they surrender a cannon they used for defense. Texas patriots answered by raising a flag which said, "Come and take it." The Mexican army never took the cannon, and today "come and take it" is the city moto.

Gonzales is also the county seat and has one of the most distinctive courthouses in the state. Built in 1896 of red brick with white trim, it is three stories high with an observation tower reaching up three stories more. It features small cupolas and turrets, clusters of columns and rounded balconies — a truly fanciful building.

On the tower is a clock with four faces, one facing each side of the square. It is not a good idea, however, to consult any one of the faces for the proper time. Not one of them is ever correct, and not one has the same time as any of the others. There is a story here, of course.

At one time, the county jail was housed beside the courthouse and prisoners on one side had a good view of the tower with its clock. One inmate, Albert Howard, had a date with the hangman for March 18, 1921. Since he claimed to be innocent of doing the murder for which he was convicted, it must have been bitter indeed to stand at the barred window of his cell and watch the hands on the big courthouse clock tick away the minutes that remained of his life.

The day arrived. As he was led away to be executed, Howard shook his fists at the clock and swore that never again would it be able to tell for sure just when a man would die.

From that very day, something seemed to go wrong with the clock. No matter how many times the repairman climbed to the top of the tower to check out the springs and dials and hands, the clock never stayed fixed. Most puzzling of all, none of the four faces ever agreed on the time.

Whether or not the malfunctioning clock had anything to do with it, Albert Howard was the last person ever to be hanged in Gonzales County.

The Thing

If you travel ten miles north of Gonzales toward San Marcos, you will reach the little town of Ottine. Here, travelers can spend some time in the Palmetto State Park, and once a year, in October, attend a festival in honor of a permanent resident of the big swamp near the park — a presence known only as "The Thing."

What is it? No one actually knows. A sighting of a gray misty shape rising from the brackish waters of the swamp has been reported. Strange, eerie cries, half-animal, half-human have been heard.

But The Thing is most often described as just a sensation that "something" is out there. Dogs react to it with a low growling in the throat, and their hair stands up along the backbone.

There are no recorded instances of The Thing ever doing any harm. It is rumored that something rocked a motor home parked near the swamp violently from side to side one night when there was no wind at all.

Many people have told of a strange, sort of psychic, knowing that The Thing is there. Tracks have been found, rather like a small hand with the thumb missing. It is believed they were made by The Thing. Some have said they think it is out there watching them, perhaps wanting to make some kind of comment, but is afraid or maybe shy.

Whatever the facts may be, The Thing has become somewhat similar to Scotland's "Nessie." The folks of Ottine have grown fond of their gentle monster and welcome visitors who would like to share this feeling.

The Ghost of Alla Hubbard

About twenty-five miles north of Dallas is the little town of Celina. On its city limits marker, it claims a population of 1,375. One ghost could be added to that number.

Just about everyone in town can tell you the story of Alla Hubbard. She moved to Collin County with her father and mother in 1866. A country doctor, Hubbard began to practice in Celina and the surrounding area. He was soon very popular with his patients.

Alla was a lovely girl in her teens — tall and slender with long brown hair and dark eyes. She was adored by her father, who wanted her to have the best of everything, including a good education.

Schools of higher learning for women were rare in those days. Although he hated the separation, Dr. Hubbard sent his daughter to Pritchett Institute in Glasgow, Missouri, which boasted a superior School of Fine Arts for young ladies.

Alla excelled in music, but that was not to be her

main interest in life. When she returned home, she was in love. At age eighteen, she had met Dr. B. F. Spencer about whom very little is known—not even whether the doctorate was medical or Ph.D. They were married, and shortly afterward, when Alla was only nineteen, she died.

It was a mysterious illness that caused her death, and Dr. Hubbard would not talk about it. Bowed down by grief, he shut himself away in his house and would see no one, although the people of the community grieved with him. The husband was gone; no one seems to know where he went.

When the doctor finally began seeing people, he was obsessed with making sure that Alla Hubbard's name never be forgotten. He had money and land, and he set about building monuments in her memory. Her husband was never mentioned.

First, a magnificent headstone of Italian marble was ordered for Alla's grave in Cottage Hill Cemetery. Flowers and greenery were planted on the plot to make her final resting place a thing of beauty. Then, Dr. Hubbard built a school and named it the Alla Hubbard School. It was four miles out of the town of Celina on the highest point of land in that part of the country.

The school was an unusual structure, built of frame and stone. Half the first floor was underground, perhaps in an effort to keep it cooler in those pre-air-conditioned days. The wide stairwell was in the center of the building, and at the landing, three large portraits were hung on the wall. These were of

Dr. Hubbard, his wife, and his beloved daughter, Alla.

Persons still living in Celina who attended the old school tell of the feeling they had when they climbed the stairs that Alla's dark eyes were following their every move. Often they raced up the stairs to the second floor to escape her stare.

The custodian of the building had stranger tales to tell. After seeing a figure of a woman in white coming down the stairs and disappearing then hearing a sound like a bowling ball bouncing down the steps, he refused to go in the school after dark.

The Superintendent of Schools who lived near the building told him that would be all right if he'd be sure to cut off all the lights before he left in the late afternoon. And although the custodian vowed that he turned the lights out every afternoon, many times the Superintendent would awaken around midnight and see lights blazing from every window.

In 1975, the Alla Hubbard School was destroyed by a tornado. The underground half of the first floor was spared as was the heavy iron bell that had been mounted on top of the building to summon the children to school each day. The three portraits were gone and never found.

The bell now sits atop a red brick foundation on a side road about four miles north of town. A large metal plaque tells the story of the Hubbard family.

It is a heavy bell of cast iron, requiring a push of strong arms to set it tolling. And yet, there are people in Celina who tell of hearing the mournful sound of the bell on clear nights when there is no wind to explain it.

The story is also told of some mischievous teenagers who planned to ring the bell as a prank one Halloween night. As they were deciding who would climb the brick monument, the lights of the sheriff's car flashed into the lane. The youths scrambled into their car, and the driver gunned the engine. They took off too fast to make the sharp turn some fifty yards down the road. The car flipped over, and the young people were injured. Consequences of an immature prank or the hand of Alla? No one cares to guess.

One last footnote to this unusual tale. If you take Texas Farm Road 455, then take the first right after the blinking light at Celina, and follow its twisting course some five or six miles, you will come to Cottage Hill Cemetery. You will notice at once the two tallest markers there. One has a beautiful carved angel at the top. That is Alla's grave; it faces east.

Next to it is a great block of granite with no ornamentation of any kind. On closer inspection, you will find that Dr. B. F. Spencer is interred there. He died in 1884, five years after his wife's death. You will also note that the grave of the husband about whom little is known, faces the west.

Little Lost Lad of Liendo

Liendo. The very name has a soft, musical, yet somehow sad sound. It is a beautiful plantation in Waller County near Hempstead — a place of tall trees dripping with Spanish moss and whispering grasses and a lovely Grecian-style home, complete with servant's quarters and carriage house. It was to Liendo that Elisabet Ney brought her family in 1872. And it was at Liendo that one of the children died.

Elisabet Ney was a strange woman. She had already made a name for herself as a fine sculptress in Europe when she suddenly closed her studio in Munich in 1870 and came to the United States, some said to escape the German military police. With her came tall, scholarly Edmund Montgomery, a successful doctor and well-known scientist. He was also Elisabet's husband, a fact she never liked to declare publicly.

They settled at Liendo after extensive travels in North America. Elisabet loved the place at first sight and expressed her feelings to the startled servants by declaiming dramatically, "Here will I live and here will I die!"

She had her own lifestyle, which included wearing flowing Grecian-style robes and striking dramatic poses from time to time. She insisted on being called by her maiden name, a practice unheard of in those times, and she treated the Texas natives with arrogance and scorn. It didn't matter to her that they laughed at her and called her a witch.

Her little boys, Lorne and Arthur, were also dressed in Grecian tunics and not allowed to mingle with the local children. Elisabet taught them herself at Liendo, and if they were lonely at times and longed for the company of people their age, she didn't seem to care.

The first few years at Liendo were trying times for Elisabet. Accustomed to hobnobbing with the aristocratic crowd in Europe, she was frustrated to find herself isolated in rural Texas with a farm to run and children to raise. She had no time for sculpting, so her career was at a standstill.

Further, her "best friend" as she called Edmund shut himself away in his study day after day, writing his scientific papers. She was probably resentful that he was getting on with his professional life while she struggled to keep the farm running.

An epidemic of diptheria swept across Texas, adding to Elisabet's trials. It is ironic that little three-year-old Arthur, living completely isolated from other children except his brother, caught the

41

disease. Horrified, Elisabet put him in the servants' quarters, a small building at the back of the main house. Cencie, who had been a combination servant and friend to the family since the days in Europe, took care of the sick child. He grew steadily worse, running a high fever and gasping for air.

Finally, little Arthur died. Elisabet wrapped the small body in a blanket and cremated him in the living room fireplace. Such a thing could not be kept secret, and rumors began to spread around the countryside. A group of men rode out from Hempstead to question the family.

Edmund faced them down. He admitted to the cremation, but insisted that Elisabet did it on orders of the doctor who feared that a simple burial would not kill the diptheria germs. When Edmund died, four years after Elisabet, the tiny urn holding the boy's ashes was placed in his coffin before he was interred.

Gossip and rumors did not die when Liendo was passed on to new owners. The plantation is said to be haunted, especially in the area where the servants' quarters used to be. Visitors have reported seeing the shadowy form of a small boy lurking under the trees. When the wind is high and the long strands of Spanish moss are whipped about, it is said that a sound like a child gasping for breath is sometimes heard as he calls piteously for his mother.

Uninvited Guests at the Governor's Mansion

It seems an unlikely residence for a ghost, the stately white-columned Governor's Mansion sitting on a slight rise to the east of the State Capitol Building in Austin. Legend has it, however, that there is certainly one, and perhaps two, other-worldly figures who have been seen and heard there.

The spirit who has been most troublesome is that of a nineteen-year-old boy, a nephew of then-Governor Pendleton Murrah. The boy had come to the Governor's Mansion for a visit and fallen hopelessly in love with the niece of Mrs. Murrah. She did not return his affections, and he was in despair.

It is possible that if Governor Murrah had not been beset by so many problems of his own, he might have offered some advice and sympathy that would help his nephew survive his broken heart. Unfortunately, Governor Murrah was ill with tuberculosis which was nearly always fatal in those days, the South was losing the war, and the state of Texas was just about broke.

43

Further, his own marriage was not a happy one. On the night he married Sue Ellen Taylor, a misunderstanding led the young groom to leave the house without his brand-new wife, and the rift was never patched up. The governor and first lady of Texas remained married in name only.

So, with no one to turn to, the boy went into the north bedroom of the Mansion on a Sunday evening in 1864, put a pistol to his head, and ended it all. Or so everyone thought.

Before very many days had passed, the bedroom became very cold—so cold that it was uncomfortable even to sleep in there at night. Also, there were sounds: deep sighs, low moans, and occasionally a cry of anguish that chilled the bones of anyone who heard it. Sometimes, there was banging on the walls and doors. The servants could not be persuaded to go in there to clean, even in bright daylight.

The Murrahs were not to be bothered by the restless spirit for long. On June 2, 1865, Texas was surrendered to the Union Army by Gen. Kirby Smith on a federal warship in Galveston Bay. Governor Murrah and other officials had to run for their lives to Mexico. Ungallantly, he left Sue Ellen behind, and she went to live with relatives in Tyler. Murrah died alone south of the Border two months later.

The ghost, too, was left behind and continued to wail and moan and bang away in the icy north bedroom. Finally, he became such a nuisance and an embarrassment when guests were present that Gov. Andrew Jackson Hamilton had the room sealed dur-

44

ing his administration as provisional governor from July 1865 to August 1866.

The room was reopened when the mansion was remodeled in 1925. Once again, visitors declared they could hear sobs of despair coming from the north bedroom, especially on Sundays—the day the boy died.

The other restless soul said to be sighted on rare occasions in the Mansion is that of Sam Houston, the hero of San Jacinto and seventh governor of the state. It is probable that the crusty old warrior had his heart broken in Austin, but not by his wife, Margaret Lea; that marriage was as steady as the Rock of Gibraltar. But by the leaders and people of the state he loved and had put his life on the line for many times.

In 1859, United States was falling apart—North against the South. A Civil War seemed unavoidable. Popular opinion in Texas went with the South and the secession of the state from the Union.

Sam disagreed. He simply couldn't conceive of his state turning its back on the United States, and he said so, again and again. It finally came down to a vote. Sam refused to declare his allegiance to the Confederacy. He remained stubbornly in his room, although he was sent for three times to cast his vote.

The office of governor of Texas was declared vacant. Sam Houston was out; he was disgraced. He packed up his wife and children and left the Governor's Mansion.

Sam died on July 26, 1863, a sad, disillusioned

old man. And soon afterward, visitors to the Governor's Mansion would sometimes catch a glimpse of a tall, stoop-shouldered figure, just outside the Houston Bedroom. It was a man in old-fashioned clothing, with wispy gray hair and sorrowful eyes, who, as they drew nearer, was no longer there.

The Unhappy Family

Today, the Jackson family would be called dysfunctional. They couldn't get along. The three grown sons, John, George, and Andrew, were constantly quarreling and sometimes coming to blows. The mother died while the boys were young and the father, Col. Sam Jackson, was much more involved with business affairs than with his boys.

In the years following the Civil War, they lived on the huge Lake Jackson Plantation on the Brazos River not far from Velasco. The main crops were cotton and sugar cane, bringing in more than enough money for the family to live in high style.

Their house was a fine southern mansion with a wide wraparound porch and tall white columns. The colonel's favorite spot when he was home was a cupola atop the second floor. He liked to pace around the small circular room with windows on all sides, declaring to anyone within hearing distance, "I own all that I can see."

The boys didn't care for work. They left that to a crew of more than seven hundred freed slaves. They preferred to hunt, fish, and make frequent trips to the gambling casinos and dance halls of New Orleans.

After the colonel died, the quarreling among the boys over who was in charge of what grew steadily worse. Finally, one day in a fit of anger, George drew his pistol and shot John in the chest, killing him instantly.

George ran away to escape punishment for what he did, but he couldn't escape from himself. Word came back that he lost his mind. He spent his final days in an institution for the insane.

Andrew was left in sole charge of the plantation, but he had no head for business, preferring instead to hunt and fish. He killed himself when his gun accidentally discharged as he was crawling through a fence.

The plantation passed into other hands and gradually went downhill. The beautiful mansion became a crumbling ruin. It still is inhabited, however. Before the cupola blew away in a storm, the bearded figure of the old colonel could often be seen there, in his favorite spot, pacing around and around and gazing out over his land.

The boys are there, too. On stormy nights, their voices can be heard, raised in angry argument. And on nights when all is still and there is no wind at all, doors slam, windows rattle, and footsteps run up and down the wide staircase.

On the spot in the yard where John was shot by his brother and lay dying, his blood staining the grass, nothing will grow. It remains a dusty brown patch of earth, the size of the fallen body of a tall man.

The Lady in Blue

Out-of-body experiences may be considered by today's television viewers as something new, brought on by the space age. According to Texas legend, this is not so.

In the 1620s, a Franciscan friar by the name of Juan de Salas ministered to the Indians of South and West Texas. He was especially loved and admired by the Jumano tribe, which lived on the Rio Concho near the site where the town of San Angelo now stands.

Friar de Salas was sent to work with the Indians when a group of them appeared at a mission near El Paso, begging for missionaries to teach them more about Christianity. The leaders of the church wondered how the Indians had heard of the Christian faith, and they pointed to a painting of a Mother Superior which hung on the walls of the mission.

"A woman who looked like this came and told us," they said.

Upon further questioning, the Indians revealed

that a young girl appeared in their midst one day, speaking to them in their own native tongue, and urging them to ask for guidance from the friars at the mission. She was dressed like the lady in the painting, they said, but her habit was a deep shade of blue.

When Friar de Salas began his teaching among the Jumanos, he was surprised to find that they already knew a great deal about the Christian faith. In answer to his questions about where they had gained such knowledge, he always heard again about the young nun dressed in blue.

A firm foundation had been laid by this mysterious teacher and Friar de Salas found his work to be easy. Before he returned to the mission, the friar baptized the chief and his entire tribe of ten thousand.

The custodian of the New Mexican area of the Catholic Church which included Texas was Father Alonzo de Benavides. Friar de Salas reported to him in detail the amazing success with the Jumanos, giving most of the credit to the Lady in Blue, although he had no idea who she might be.

When Father Benavides was ordered to return to Spain to report on his work in the New World, he spoke of the conversion of the Jumano tribe and mentioned the fine missionary work done by the Lady in Blue. His supervisors were extremely pleased but not in the least surprised.

Father Benavides was sent to the small town of Agreda on the Spanish border and introduced to

Mother Maria de Jesus. She was a handsome woman in her late twenties, wearing the traditional habit of the nuns of her convent, the cloak of which was a deep blue. She told Father Benavides an amazing story.

She was born Maria Fernandez Coronel in 1602 and by the time she was in her teens was deeply religious and realized she had a strange power. She could go into a trancelike state during which her soul floated out of her body and traveled to a wild land inhabited by savage natives with reddish-brown skin and dark hair and eyes.

She preached the gospel to these people and they responded to her as though they understood, even though she spoke in Spanish. She told them about Jesus and Mary and eternal life if they converted to Christianity and were baptized. According to Mother Maria, she made as many as five hundred visitations to the Texas Indians between 1620 and 1631, beginning when she was only eighteen years old.

Mother Maria's story was known among the members of the Catholic Church in Spain and Father Benavides' report of a Lady in Blue among the Indians in Texas served to authenticate it. Later missionaries in Texas heard of her from natives who knew about the Christian faith, although Mother Maria stated that she made no visitations to the New World after 1631.

As is the case with many unexplainable phenomena, the story of the Lady in Blue has slipped into the category of legend or even myth. There are even stories of a ghostly figure wearing transparent blue garments, wandering through the historic streets of Nacogdoches in East Texas, and weeping for the vanished Indian tribes she came to save.

Who is to say? The facts of the story have been documented in historic accounts. There was, indeed, a Maria de Agreda, a deeply religious nun who wore a blue cloak and never left her native Spain. There were, indeed, primitive tribes of Indians in Texas, across an ocean from Spain, who somehow learned the doctrines and rites of the Christian faith before the Spanish friars arrived to teach them. As for the rest, perhaps it should be left for each individual to decide just how this could have happened.

The Woman of the Western Star

In 1844, the frontier of Texas was a dangerous place to be. There were constant battles between the Indians and Texans, with many casualties on both sides.

The hills around Bandera were favored by marauding Indian bands, and the settlers at Polley's Peak lived in fear of unexpected attacks. The Texas Rangers were sent to clear out the hostile warriors, and scarcely a day went by that there wasn't a skirmish. After a few weeks, the Rangers were tired and weary of fighting.

One night, they sat around the campfire. It was still and cold, and occasionally they heard the distant call of a whippoorwill. This sent chills up their spines, for the Indians often signaled to one another with bird calls. The men stared into the fire and thought of home.

The night was dark, with clouds covering the moon and a sort of mist rising from the ground. Suddenly, the clouds parted and a great radiance

hung over the campsite. Into it stepped a tall, beautiful Indian maiden. She wore a robe the color of the blue sky and a shawl like a rainbow. On her dark braided hair sat a circlet of beads that sparkled like diamonds. A jeweled quiver hung at her side.

The Rangers reached for their weapons, certain the woman had been sent to distract them from an impending attack.

The captain stood. "Wait a minute, men," he said. Then he faced the maiden. "Who are you? Where do you come from, and why are you here?"

The woman spoke and her voice was clear and musical. "I am the Woman of the Western Star. I come to make straight the path between my people and yours. We are tired of fighting. No more blood must be shed. There must be peace."

The captain frowned. "But weren't you afraid to come here alone to the camp of the enemy?"

"No. I am protected by the Great Spirit, my father."

From the quiver at her side, the woman drew three polished arrows and laid them at her feet. Then, she turned and faced the west, pointing to a bright star. "That is my home. I go there now."

There was a flash of bright light and the men shaded their eyes. When they looked again, the Indian maiden was gone. And so were the arrows.

No warriors came that night, and no marauding bands were encountered the next day. Soon, the settlers at Polley's Peak began to feel safe in their homes. The Indians who came and went no longer bothered them.

Many of the Indians made a pilgrimage to a high cliff above Bandera Pass where a beloved old Chief was buried. To thank him for sending the Woman of the Western Star and bringing peace, they placed arrowheads and pretty stones on his grave. It is all still there.

The Rangers who were present when the Woman of the Western Star appeared passed the story down to their families and it has become a familiar Texas legend.

"Oonie"

In the little town of Karnack near the Texas-Louisiana border, there is a beautiful mansion built of red brick. It was designed in the mid-1800s for Maj. Milt Andrews who ran a general store in Port Caddo. He called it The Brick House.

Through the years, it has been a busy house. Tragic, strange, and wonderful things have happened there.

Major Andrews had a beautiful daughter named Eunice. One night she was sitting by the fireplace in her upstairs bedroom. A fierce storm was raging outside, and a bolt of lightning came down the chimney, struck her, and killed her.

Heartbroken, the father sold the house and moved, but it is said that the spirit of Eunice stayed. Visitors to the house told of hearing the sound of a woman weeping coming from the room where Eunice died.

An eccentric doctor bought the house. For some reason, he filled one of the rooms floor to ceiling with hickory nuts. These were still in place when T. J. (Cap) Taylor purchased The Brick House for his bride, Minnie, in 1904. The Taylors were from Alabama. T. J. went into the merchandising business, starting out with a general store in Karnack where he sold any and everything people in that area might need.

It was now that something wonderful happened in the red brick house. A beautiful baby girl was born to T. J. and Minnie. They named her Claudia, but one of the servants declared the child to be so pretty she was like a little Lady Bird. The nickname caught on. Future First Lady Ladybird Johnson spent her early childhood in Karnack.

Then tragedy struck again. Minnie had a bad fall on the stairs and never recovered. She died when Ladybird was very young.

The Brick House has stayed in the Taylor family. Jerry Jones, a nephew of T. J.'s second wife lives there now with his family and manages the farm. It is through young Jett Jones, Jerry's son, that the story of the ghost of Eunice Andrews has been reborn.

When Jett was about two, he began to talk about a playmate no one could see but him. His name for her was "Oonie."

As he grew older, he talked about "Oonie" quite naturally and told everyone she was a pretty girl in a white dress. It wasn't frightening or strange to him at all that he had a friend who was invisible to everyone else. It wasn't lost on anyone that the name "Oonie" could be a childish nickname for Eunice.

Jett was close to his older sister, Angela, and he told her that "Oonie" had a hot temper and sometimes threw things around, but she was usually sweet and kind. Whether or not it was the power of suggestion, Angela admitted to hearing a girl's voice in the upstairs bedroom from time to time, but she never shared her brother's close friendship with "Oonie."

In his book, *Texas*, Frank X. Tolbert tells of a night he spent in Eunice's room at the invitation of young Jett. Around midnight, a window shade suddenly rolled to the top with a loud sound. He pulled it back down. The next morning, sunlight was shining through a tear in the shade that hadn't been there the night before. Also, he heard shuffling sounds in an adjoining bathroom during the night, but when he investigated, no one was there. Mr. Tolbert admitted it was nice to get out in the bright daylight the next morning.

Knowledge of "Oonie" is quite general both in Karnack and its neighboring Jefferson, which boasts a few ghostly spirits of its own.

The Roomers
in the Ranch House

The phone call came around nine P.M. A near-hysterical voice on the other end cried, "I think we have ghosts in the bedroom!"

The call was received by Nancy Schmidt, a Dallas businesswoman. At the time, however, she lived in the West Texas city of El Paso with her seventeen-year-old daughter, Lynda. The call was made by Nancy's friend, Meg, a retired schoolteacher who lived with her retired-engineer husband, Harvey, on the outskirts of town.

They had restored a beautiful old ranch house dating back to the cattle days of El Paso del Norte. It was a place of twelve-foot ceilings, great stone fireplaces, and large airy rooms — certainly not a place that would encourage ghostly beings. Nancy thought Meg must be pulling her leg and said so.

"No, I'm serious," Meg replied. "All of a sudden, there are strange noises we can't explain — and other things. I've even felt the touch of a cold hand, sort of an electric shock sensation. We're at our wit's end."

She begged Nancy to come out to see if she could hear and see the things as well. More to humor her good friend than anything else, Nancy agreed. When she mentioned the ghosts to Lynda, she insisted on going along, wondering aloud if Nancy's friends might have had a bit too much of the grape.

"You know they don't drink," Nancy said, sternly. "I don't know what's going on out there, but something is."

Meg was standing on the front porch when they got there. With her was one of the beautiful collie dogs she and Harvey raised to show.

"Whatever this is, it's in the bedroom, just off the parlor," she told Nancy. She suggested that they take the dog in with them to see how he would react.

When they reached the bedroom door, the dog refused to enter the room. He planted his four feet firmly on the floor and resisted every effort to get him into the bedroom.

The first thing Nancy noticed when they went in was the bone-chilling cold. It was August and the house was air-conditioned, but this was the cold of a freezer chest. Over by the window was an old-fashioned rocking chair. It was slowly and rhythmically rocking back and forth, back and forth, even though no one was in it.

On the bed was an impression like one made when someone lies down on top of the spread. Meg insisted no one had occupied the room for a long

62

time. Occasionally, the curtain at the window rippled as though someone was passing by. And there were noises—bumps and moans and sighs.

All of a sudden, Lynda jumped. "Something touched me!" she cried. "On the back of my neck—cold and sort of like a mild electric shock."

That startled Nancy. Although Meg had mentioned the feeling of being touched, Nancy had not said anything about it to her daughter.

There was no sense of evil or danger in the room—just the discomfort of "something" being present that no one could identify or explain. Nancy and Lynda were happy to leave, and Lynda locked all the car doors in case whatever-it-was decided to go home with them.

The next week, Meg called in a priest from New Mexico to "purify" the house. That was a mistake. All he succeeded in doing was to drive the presence out of just one room and into the rest of the house. Now the wails and groans and bumps could be heard all over.

Meg and Harvey loved the old house and didn't want to move. Somehow, they were able to communicate this feeling to the ghostly beings and suggested that they try to just peacefully coexist. Soon afterward, the presence returned to the bedroom and has been there exclusively ever since.

A local historian dug up the fact that the site where the ranch house stands was once an Indian burial ground. Through the long years, it had been lost and didn't appear on any maps as a historical or protected location.

When the water company dug trenches to pipe water to the house, it is possible they crossed through the burial ground and disturbed Indian spirits that had long occupied that place. This was offered to Meg and Harvey as an explanation for the strange happenings at their house.

Nancy went out to play cards with her friends one night. The game was laid out on the parlor table. In the adjacent bedroom, Nancy could hear faint sighs and groans, and the creak of a rocking chair. Everyone just ignored it. Seemed the strange occupants in the bedroom were there to stay.

The Enchanted Rock
of Llano County

It is a place sacred to the Indians. For centuries they came from miles away to have their ceremonies, some of which, in earlier days, included human sacrifice.

This Enchanted Rock covers six hundred forty acres in Llano County, not far from Fredericksburg. It is a huge mound of granite, with flecks on the surface that glitter like glass in the sunlight. At night, strange lights seem to crackle and burn here and there, a thing called spirit fires by the Indians. When it rains, the streams of water pouring down the sides look like molten silver.

According to Indian legend, somewhere in the rock is a mine of pure silver. It is protected by the spirits of an ancient Indian tribe which used the rock as a fortress against their enemies.

In the early days of Texas, the Comanche Indians had rituals at the rock. When they lost a battle and many braves were killed, or a natural disaster like a drought or a flood occurred, they thought the

Spirit of the Rock was angry. It was then they offered a human sacrifice, sometimes a girl captured from one of the settlements.

At one time, a young soldier of fortune from Spain, Don Jesus Navarro, came to the Mission San Jose near San Antonio. He stayed to help with the defense against a large band of Comanches said to be gathering for an attack on the mission.

Here, also, lived an Indian chief, Tehuan, and his daughter who was called Rosa. The two young people met and fell in love.

Within a few days, the Indians attacked. During the fierce battle, Navarro was stunned by a tomahawk blow to his head. He lay in the tall grass, unconscious for a long while. When his senses returned, the battle was over and the Indians had retreated. To his horror, Navarro discovered they had taken Rosa with them.

The men at the mission were exhausted and many of them were wounded, so Navarro leaped on his horse and rode to Goliad to recruit some men to help him rescue his sweetheart. They traveled fast, and soon discovered the large Indian camp.

The Texans in the group realized the Comanches were probably headed for the Enchanted Rock, possibly planning to sacrifice Rosa to the Spirit of the Rock. They didn't share their suspicions with Navarro for fear he would ruin all chances of rescuing Rosa by doing something rash.

Instead, they told him that the rock was a sacred place to the Indians and would be a good spot

to attack while they were busy with their ritual ceremonies. They followed the Indians for the next few days, staying far enough behind to avoid discovery.

Somehow, they got a little too far behind and by the time they reached the Rock, the Comanches had already tied Rosa to a stake and were piling pieces of wood around her. Quickly, Navarro divided his men into two groups, and they attacked from both sides. The Indians were caught totally by surprise. When they turned to defend themselves, Navarro rode swiftly to Rosa's side, cut the leather thongs that bound her, and swung her up behind him on his horse.

Instead of riding through the battle, he then guided his horse up onto the rock. For a moment, the Indians stared, amazed. No one had ever dared step on the rock, much less ride a horse on its surface. Certain the Spirit of the Rock would instantly destroy them all, the Indians ran for their lives into the forest.

Rosa was saved—by the Enchanted Rock!

The Little Ghost Girl

In 1986, when well-known Texas storyteller, Finley Stewart and his fiancee, Sylvia Pitchford moved into a big loft apartment over a store on the square in downtown Denton, they thought it would be exciting to renovate the old place. They didn't know how exciting.

The apartment was divided into two separate areas by a pair of heavy wooden doors. The only entry was up a flight of stairs and through a single side door. Light came in from two large windows in the front looking out over the square and a similar pair on the back wall, overlooking a sudden drop to the ground below. The front windows were sealed shut, making the room very hot.

The original walls of the apartment were brick, but a former tenant had covered them over with white plaster. The young couple thought the brick more desirable, so before they moved in, they began scraping away the plaster.

When they quit working that night, they left a

rather thick coating of powdered plaster on the floor. The next morning when they returned, they saw a trail of very clear prints of a small child's bare feet, beginning at the front windows, proceeding through the heavy double doors, and fading out near the back window where there was no powder.

This was quite puzzling, but the young folks went ahead with their work and moved in a few days later with their two dogs, miniature Australian sheepdogs named Bemougeot and Rags.

One night, Bemougeot suddenly sat up straight and stared at the door. A moment later, it banged open. The dog got up and headed for the back as though he were following someone.

The walls in the back area were quite old, and the floor was covered with a cracked linoleum that had been nailed down. Bemougeot began to whine and claw at the floor covering, and succeeded in tearing a small rip in it. When Finley peeled back the linoleum, he found a tintype photo of the kind popular around the turn of the century. It was of a pretty little girl about five years old wearing an old-fashioned white dress.

Sylvia's interest was really piqued now. She went to the courthouse to look in old records to find who had lived in the apartment at that time. She learned that a dry goods store had occupied the second floor of the building around 1900, and the family who owned it lived in rooms behind the store. They had a little five-year-old girl. No names were given, so Finley and Sylvia decided to call their ghostly little resident Clara.

They were always being reminded that she was there. Sometimes, when Finley was working at his desk at night, he could clearly hear the childish sing-song voice of a little girl, rattling off some kind of story. But he couldn't understand what she was saying. It is very quiet in downtown Denton at night, and he was certain the voice didn't come from the street.

Another time, Sylvia called in a startled voice from the back area for Finley to look. What he saw was a circle of light, revolving, but moving toward the front of the apartment at a measured pace. It passed through the double doors and disappeared out the front windows—the ones that were sealed shut.

In the kitchen area, which was the hottest part of the apartment, from time to time there were spots that were extremely cold. The last manifestation of Clara's presence was a thick coating of green, evil-smelling mold that appeared on a kitchen counter. In a few hours it was gone. It returned once more the next day, and when it disappeared once again, that was the last they saw or heard of Clara.

For a year and a half, they were aware of the little girl's presence, but never once did they feel she was anything but sweet and gentle. They never felt threatened in any way and sometimes admitted that they missed their little girl ghost.

The Lady in the Gray Dress

Back in the mid-1800s, a couple moved into a large two-story house near the West Texas town of Childress. The man was tall and well-dressed and carried himself like a soldier. The woman, too, was tall and slender and always wore an old-fashioned dress of shiny gray material whose full skirt swept the ground.

For the first few days after their arrival, the couple did not set foot outside the house. The ladies of the church decided to pay them a visit, as was their custom on the rare occasions when someone new moved to town.

The man answered their knock and invited them in. He had a courtly manner as he led them into a tastefully furnished parlor.

"My name is Hughbert," he told them. "And my wife, Abigail, will be down shortly."

Just then, the woman came down the stairs, wearing the long gray dress. Nodding brusquely to the visitors, she went to each window in the room, closed it, and then went back up the stairs.

The visitors were taken aback by her rude behavior and said they must go. Hughbert showed them to the door in his gentlemanly manner, but he didn't ask them to come again.

Every morning after that, Hughbert could be seen walking into town to get a paper, check the post, and pick up a few supplies. He was always immaculately dressed and spoke to people he met in a friendly way.

The only time Abigail was seen was when she made her rounds several times a day, closing the windows. The people shook their heads because no one could ever remember seeing the windows open.

Hughbert was not seen in town for several days. Fearing that he might be ill and that his wife needed help, the pastor of the church went to the two-story house and knocked on the door. After a long time, Abigail opened it just a crack and peered out.

"I came to inquire about Hughbert," the pastor said. "Is he all right?"

"Hughbert has gone away," Abigail said and closed the door.

The neighbors didn't know what to think about this strange couple. Abigail had asked for no help, however, and could still be seen closing the windows several times a day. They assumed she was doing all right on her own and tried to quit worrying about her.

After a few days, the house appeared to be empty. The shadowy gray figure of Abigail was no longer seen going from window to window.

The neighbors contacted the owner of the house,

and suggested that he check on his renters. He did, and he found the house empty. There was no sign of either Abigail or Hughbert, but the house was neat and clean. Strangely enough, the windows were all open.

Assuming the couple had just moved on, the owner locked up the house, put a "For Rent" sign in the yard, and went on with his business. What his tenants chose to do was not his concern, as long as they paid their rent and took care of the property.

After a time, the house was rented to a middle-aged couple who had a young niece living with them. Different from Hughbert and Abigail, these people were friendly and outgoing, and soon they got to know their neighbors. They were told the story of the former tenants, of course, but seemed to find it amusing rather than mysterious and weird.

At some distance behind the house was a stock pond. One day, the niece heard her dog barking and went to get him. He was on the bank of the pond, barking loudly.

The young girl was horrified to see, just beneath the surface of the water, a woman in a gray dress, staring up at her through the rippling water. She was dead.

The girl ran screaming to the house, and soon the sheriff was being led to the pond. He found nothing. There was no body in the spot pointed out by the girl, and days of dragging the pond produced nothing. The incident was dismissed as a product of an overactive imagination, induced by the story of Abigail.

Several days afterward, the niece returned home from school to find that her aunt and uncle were not there. As she started up to her room, she saw a woman, wearing a long, gray dress, coming down the stairs, her arms outstretched.

"What a dear little girl," the woman said. "I have always wanted a sweet child like you."

The girl recognized the woman as the body in the pond. She ran from the house and nothing could persuade her to return. This time, her story was believed.

The family packed up and moved away. No one in the town would go near the house, convinced it was haunted. Even the owner abandoned the place and allowed it to become run-down from neglect.

One night during an electrical storm, a bolt of lightning struck the house and part of it burned. The section where the parlor had been remained standing. Persons in the community declared that on some nights, they could see a shadowy figure dressed in gray moving about inside the parlor, shutting down each window in turn.

Haunted Bridges

As the waters of rivers and lakes and swamps furnish the settings for many Texas ghost tales, so do the bridges which span them. The schoolchildren of the towns of Giddings and Silsbee tell the story of "Crybaby Bridge," each group claiming its location to be in the countryside nearby. That's how it is with folktales.

The story goes that a young mother was abandoned by her husband and her family. Left alone with no resources and a sickly infant who cried constantly, she soon became distraught. Finally, she got into her car and drove it into the country. Midway across a bridge, she flung the child into the dark waters below.

Here, the stories differ about whether she, too, jumped from the bridge and was drowned, or just disappeared. At any rate, neither mother nor child was ever seen again.

It is said now that on certain nights when the moon is full and the wind is making a moaning sound in the trees, persons crossing the bridge are startled by the sound of a crying infant coming from the water below. Some of them, not knowing the story about the bridge, have summoned help, only to be told that it is not a living child they hear. Rather, it is the restless spirit of a baby drowned by its mother many years ago.

Another haunted bridge called "The Screaming Bridge" has an urban location. It spans the Trinity River on the Arlington Bedford Road and was the site where four teenaged girls drowned many years ago. The cause of the accident is not known, but friends of the girls said they had planned to visit the Pleasant Valley Cemetery in Cedar Hill earlier in the night.

This particular graveyard has a reputation among young folk of the Metroplex area for ghostly and bizarre happenings. The Cedar Hill police have to patrol the vicinity constantly to keep away thrill-seeking teens and the more dangerous followers of cults who want to perform their rituals in the eerie atmosphere.

It is not known what happened to the girls or what they may have seen or imagined in their visit to the cemetery. They were traveling at a high speed and may have been upset or frightened when their car ran off the bridge. Nevertheless, all of them were drowned.

Now, some of the people who live near the bridge claim that on still, dark nights, similar to the one of the accident, they can see the headlights of the car plummeting through the air and hear the screams of the doomed teenagers. These are the folks who gave the name to "The Screaming Bridge."

The Haunted Stagecoach Stations

One of the regular stops on the old Butterfield Stagecoach route through Texas in the late 1800s was a big two-story building on a high rocky hill in the little community of Possum Kingdom. Often, passengers who were on a long journey would stop over to rest a few days until another stage came along.

With the coming of the Iron Horse, travel by stagecoach became a thing of the past. Some of the stations continued to operate for a time as hotels and boarding houses, but most were eventually abandoned or turned into family dwellings.

Such was the case with the large building at Possum Kingdom. It stood lonely and unoccupied for many years. Then, the York family came to Texas and bought the old station for their home.

The York family was large, with many children. Still, there were more rooms in the old building than they needed. Some of the rooms were closed and never used.

Each night, it was someone's responsibility to

make the rounds of the empty rooms to make sure the doors were shut tightly before the family retired. Each morning, however, the door to one certain room would be ajar.

At first, the Yorks thought nothing of it. Perhaps there was a draft that caused the door to open. But when they continued to see it standing open morning after morning when it was closed tightly the night before, they began to wonder. Could someone be slipping in to sleep in the room and leaving before the family awoke the next morning? It was disquieting to think someone they didn't know at all might be under the same roof with them every night.

Mr. York bought some strong baling wire and some heavy duty nails. The wire made the door all but impossible to open. And yet, the next morning, with unbelieving eyes, they saw the door standing open.

Truly concerned now, Mr. York began to ask old-timers in the community about the history of the station. What he found out didn't ease his mind at all. In fact, he began to look for another place to live.

The story went that a man stopped off at the station one night with plans to stay a few days before he continued with his journey. When he didn't show up for breakfast the next morning, the station master went to his room to awaken him.

He found the room awash in blood, the floors and walls splattered with red as though there had been a terrible fight. Lying on the floor with his throat slit was the man who had checked in the night before.

No one knew who he was, and there were no papers of any kind in his carpet bag to identify him. After a vain search to locate any relatives or friends, the man was buried in a pauper's grave and soon forgotten. His room had been the one with the door that would not stay closed.

The Yorks could not help but wonder if they had a restless ghost — the spirit of a murdered man whose killer was never punished and who lay in an unmarked grave far away from family or friends — under their roof every night.

They moved away and again the old building stood vacant, except perhaps for the nightly visitor, seeking no one knows what. Eventually, the old building was torn down, but the York family has passed the story of the door that would not stay closed from generation to generation.

A family that moved into the old stagecoach station at Bee Cave, Texas, had a similar eerie experience. A few nights after they had settled into their new home, they were awakened by the sound of horses' hooves and carriage wheels moving into the gravel courtyard in front of the house. The father sent the oldest son down to find out who the unexpected visitors might be.

Soon, the boy returned with a puzzled expression on his face.

"No one's there, Father," he said. "But there were tracks of carriage wheels in the gravel."

"Perhaps they realized they had come to the wrong place and drove on," the father answered, and herded his family back to bed.

A few nights later, they heard the horse and carriage again. This time, after a few moments, the front door of the house opened and the sound of voices in conversation floated up the stairs.

More angry than frightened, the father picked up his rifle from beside the bed and thundered down the stairs. "Who's there?" he bellowed. "How dare you trespass into my home?"

He flung open the door to the parlor to find it empty of anything but furniture. He rushed through the door and out to the porch. Nothing was there, but very clear in the bright moonlight were the indentations of carriage wheels in the gravel of the courtyard.

The next day, he talked to the people of the community, seeking an answer to the mystery. No one could tell him why he was having the strange midnight visits.

Declaring the old station to be haunted, the family moved away. Now, many people visit the old house, hoping to hear the sounds of the ghostly carriage and its occupants. And some of them come away, claiming that they did.

The Wandering Spirit
of Moses Rose

On the monument to heroes of the Alamo on the grounds of the state capitol, there is an error. Listed among those who gallantly fought and died in that historic battle is one L. M. Rose. Louie "Moses" Rose was at the Alamo, true, but he chose not to stay and fight.

Rose was a good friend of Jim Bowie. He had immigrated from France after fighting in the Napoleonic wars and was ready to put down roots and become a farmer in Texas. He just happened to be visiting his friend at the Alamo when Santa Anna attacked and began the siege.

When Travis drew the line on the floor of the Alamo and asked all who would stay, fight, and face almost certain death to cross the line, Rose hung back in the shadows. All the other men crossed over.

Later, when the men had returned to their posts, Rose crept in to see his friend who was lying on a cot, very ill with a fever.

"This is not my fight, Jim," he said. "I'm a

Frenchman, and I've had enough of war. I just want to live out my days in peace."

"Do what your conscience tells you, old friend," Jim replied. "And God go with you."

It was not at all certain that Rose could get away from the Alamo. Santa Anna's men were everywhere. But after the moon set and the night was very dark, Rose climbed the wall of the Alamo and dropped over the side. Crawling on his belly through the bodies of dead soldiers and moving slowly to avoid the sentries, he made his slow, tortuous way to freedom.

Trying not to think about what happened to the men he left behind at the Alamo, Moses Rose attempted to make a new life for himself. And then, someone learned what he had done and his story was told in the *Texas Almanac* of 1873. After that, no one wanted anything to do with him. He tried many trades, but when his identity was discovered, his businesses failed. He finally lost everything — money, friends, family.

A farming family near the town of Logansport took him in, and he stayed with them, doing odd jobs for food and shelter. There is a street in the town named Castoff Street which many say was named for Rose who was certainly a castoff in Texas.

Rose died sometime in the late 1800s; no one is certain of the exact date. Also, the location of his grave is not known. There is a soapstone marker in a cemetery between Rusk and Alto bearing the name "Moses Rose."

83

Whether or not the body of Moses Rose lies in that grave is not known for sure, but some old-timers are certain that his spirit is not at rest. They say it wanders restlessly back and forth, seeking someone who will welcome him and forgive him for deserting his friends at the Alamo. No one has actually seen the ghost of Moses Rose, but his presence can be felt at times quite strongly along the streams and in the woods of Southeast Texas, where he lived out his last lonely years as an outcast.

Of Lafitte and LaPorte

The old Beazley house near LaPorte was said to be haunted. The story is told of a Civil War soldier returning home by horseback who found himself by the large vacant house as darkness fell. He was bone-tired and decided to spend the night in one of the empty rooms.

He fell into a deep sleep, but near midnight he was awakened by a noise. Something was in the room with him. He opened his eyes to see a figure standing near him — a pirate with a fierce bearded face and piercing eyes. The soldier sat up, shocked and frightened.

"W-who are you?" he asked, shakily.

"I am the ghost of Jean Lafitte," the man said in deep, hollow tones that seemed to echo through the room. "Under this floor is buried more treasure than is good for any man. I am doomed to remain here and guard it from the evil forces who would come to take it from me."

"Please, sir," the soldier said, his voice shaking.

"I am not here to steal your treasure. I only wanted a place to sleep for the night."

"Then you have nothing to fear," said the pirate. And then he was gone, fading into a shaft of moonlight through the window.

The soldier snatched up his knapsack, ran for his horse, and rode away as though the devil himself were chasing him. He told the story to friends and family, but they dismissed it as the imagination of a war-weary mind.

Somehow, the word spread that there was buried treasure under the old house, and treasure hunters came seeking it. One such man was digging around the foundations of the old place, and before he knew it, night was upon him. He was very tired and decided to rest a bit before starting out for home.

He fell asleep, and when he awoke it was a black midnight. As he rubbed the sleep from his eyes, he noticed a sort of glow, coming from the spot where he had been digging earlier. As he stared, the figure of a woman emerged, dressed in long, flowing, old-fashioned clothing.

Before he could scramble to his feet and run, the woman spoke to him.

"I am Theodosia Burr," she told him. "I am here to guard the treasure of my lord and master, Jean Lafitte. There is no need for you to search further. You cannot find the treasure unless I show you, and that I will never do." Her eyes glared at him fiercely.

Shaking with fear, the man gathered his tools and ran away into the night. He would not seek help from a ghost, no matter who she might be.

A few days later when the man had recovered from his fright, he was overcome by curiosity. He went to the history section of the public library to see what he could find out about Theodosia Burr.

He learned that she was the daughter of the traitor, Aaron Burr. She was lost at sea in 1812, and her body was never found. The treasure hunter recalled stories of a mysterious lady who was the mistress of the large red brick house, Maison Rouge, built by Jean Lafitte on Galveston Island. She never appeared in public, and no one really knows who she was.

Could it be, he thought, *that she was Theodosia Burr*. Perhaps she had been captured at sea by Lafitte and carried off to his palatial home.

The old Beazley house is no longer there. In the 1900s it was destroyed by a lightning strike. But though the house is gone, the stories of pirates, their ladies, and a treasure trove of buried gold and jewels live on.